The Secret Slide

# Trouble at the Toy Store

Published by B&H Publishing Group

Nashville, Tennessee

Scripture is taken from New Living Translation, copyright © 1996, 2004, 2015 by Tyndale House Foundation. Used by permission of Tyndale House Publishers, Inc., Carol Stream, Illinois 60188. All rights reserved.

Dewey Decimal Classification: JF

Subject Heading: PERSONAL FINANCE / SAVING AND INVESTMENT / STEWARDSHIP

1 2 3 4 5 6 7 • 22 21 20 19

To my sons—Nathaniel,

Joshua, and James

# Contents

# Read This First!

This is the story about Jake, Sophia, and Brody. They have a really big challenge—to rescue people from a mean and selfish villain named Albatross. (Say it with me: *AL-ba-tross.*)

Jake, Sophia, and Brody travel down a secret slide that changes them into agents for the Secret Slide Money Club.

Wait—they are not agents yet. They have to complete three challenges to become agents.

And guess what? They have already completed two! Pretty cool, right?

So, that means this book is about their third challenge. You picked a really good book to read!

I hope they finish it. If they fail, no more secret slide for them. That would stink like an Albie (say it with me: *AL-bee*). They smell like dirty, wet socks. Gross.

By the way, Albies are people who have to do whatever Albatross tells them to do. They got that way by making bad money choices and not following the Master's Money Plan (Give—Save—Live).

But you already knew that. So anyway . . .

Jake, Sophia, and Brody are in gym class right now. But before we jump into the class, let me give you a quick tip—LOOK OUT!

# Chapter 1
# Look Out!!!

LOOK OUT, BRODY!" Sophia yelled.

Brody ducked, and the ball flew over his head.

"Whew! That was close!" Brody said. "Thanks, Sophia."

Jake, Sophia, and Brody were in gym class at school. Today they were playing dodgeball.

The three friends were the last ones left on their side. Two other classmates were on the other side.

Jake threw a ball at a classmate. "I love this class!" Jake said. "WATCH OUT, SOPHIA!"

A ball was about to hit Sophia. She jumped out of the way.

She shook her head. "This is not my idea of fun."

Sophia had just stopped talking when a ball hit her.

"HEY!" Sophia said.

Mr. Ratt, the gym teacher, blew his whistle. *TWEEEET!!!* "You are out, Sophia. Go sit down."

Sophia mumbled to herself, "Good. I didn't like that game anyway." She sat by the gym wall and started reading a book.

Now there were only two players on each side. Jake and Brody looked at each other.

"We can do this. Let's go," Jake said.

Jake and Brody each picked up a ball. They ran toward the other team. Their two classmates each picked up a ball. They ran toward Jake and Brody.

Then Brody smelled something. He stopped running and held his nose. "Ewww!"

Jake turned around. "What?"

*BAMMMM!!!*

*POWWWW!!!*

"AAAHHHH!" Jake and Brody yelled.

They both had been hit by balls. They fell to the ground.

Mr. Ratt blew his whistle. *TWEEEET!!!* "Jake and Brody are out. Game over!"

Jake could not believe it. They had never lost at dodgeball.

"Why did you stop?" he asked Brody.

"I thought I smelled something," Brody said. "It smelled like an Albie."

Jake sighed. "Could you not wait until after we won dodgeball?" asked Jake.

Sophia walked over to Jake and Brody. She helped them off the ground.

"You know that stopping makes you an easy target," she said.

Jake rolled his eyes. "Yes, I know," Jake said. "Brody stopped because he thought he smelled an Albie."

"Sorry, Jake," Brody said. "I really thought I did."

Jake, Sophia, and Brody went over to the side of the gym. Their friend Marcus was there.

"Hey, guys," Marcus said. "You know the game is called dodgeball because you have to DODGE the balls."

"We know," Jake said.

Marcus smiled. "You all should come over to my house tomorrow. I'm getting the new *Super Dodgeball 3* video game tonight!"

Brody was excited. "No way! That game is fun!"

"I bet I would like it better than real dodgeball," Sophia said. "That game costs a lot. How do you have enough money?"

"I saved my money," Marcus said. "I also got this ad in the mail."

Marcus reached in his backpack. He pulled out an ad from Terry's Toy Store.

"EWW!!!" Jake said. The three friends held their noses.

Marcus nodded. "The ad does stink. It smells like dirty, wet socks. Weird."

Jake, Sophia, and Brody looked at the ad. It read,

**Super Surprise! Today Only! Don't Miss It!**

The class bell rang. Marcus put the ad back in his backpack.

"I have to go," Marcus said. "See you tomorrow!"

As Marcus left, the three friends looked at each other.

"Why would that ad smell like an Albie?" Sophia asked.

"I don't know," Jake said. "But something is not right."

The friends' watches made a pinging noise. It was Agent G.B.

"WOOHOO!" Jake said. "Our third challenge!"

Jake gave Sophia and Brody a high five.

"See you two at the slide after school," Jake said.

Sophia took out her notebook. She always took good notes. Sophia wrote,

*Marcus's ad smells like an Albie. YUCK!*

# Chapter 2
# Slide Time

Where is he?" Sophia asked.

Jake and Sophia were at the Oak City Park playground. They looked at their watches. Brody should have been there.

"Ugh. He is always late," Jake said.

"Hey, do you hear that?" asked Sophia.

It was an ice cream truck. The truck played music as it drove past.

"Hmm. . . . I have a feeling that Brody isn't far away," Sophia said.

Sure enough, Brody came running down the street. He was waving his arms at the ice cream truck. The driver did not see him.

"Ah, man!" Brody said. "I chased him for two miles!"

"Really?" Jake asked.

"Everybody needs goals," Brody said.

"You care more about the ice cream truck than about being late?" asked Sophia. "I don't get you."

Brody thought for a second. "Well . . . have you tried the chocolate-dipped ice cream bar? It's so good."

Sophia shook her head.

A small door at the top of the tube slide started glowing green.

"Come on. Let's go," Jake said.

The three friends went up to the slide. Jake placed his hand on the door. It opened to show three buttons on a control panel. Each button had a word above it—GIVE, SAVE, and LIVE.

"I got it!" Brody said.

Brody pushed the GIVE button.

*DING!!!*

He then pushed the LIVE button.

*ERRRRRRRR!!!*

"Brody, you know the pattern," Sophia said. She pulled out her notebook. "Look."

### *GIVE—SAVE—LIVE*

"Oh, yeah," Brody said.

He pushed the buttons in order: GIVE—
SAVE—LIVE.

*DING!!! DING!!! DING!!!*

The inside of the tube slide started glowing green. Jake jumped down the slide.

"WOOHOOOOOO!"

Brody went after Jake.

"YEEEAAAHHH!"

Sophia sat down on the slide. She slowly pushed herself down the slide.

"YIIIIIIKES!"

The three friends went round, round, and underground. As they sped down, down, down, their clothes were transformed into black suits, green ties, and really cool sunglasses.

Jake and Brody flipped out onto the floor of the Secret Slide Money Club headquarters. Sophia slowly came to the end of the slide and stood up.

Jake smiled. "Now, that was better than a chocolate-dipped ice cream bar! Right, Brody?"

Sophia was laughing. She pointed at Brody. "He's not thinking about ice cream bars!"

"Brody, what is on your hand?" Jake asked.

Brody shook his head. "Umm . . . I think it's an oven mitt." Brody yelled at the slide, "WHY DON'T YOU LIKE ME?!"

Now Jake was laughing. "What's cooking, Brody?"

"Not funny," Brody said. "It won't come off."

Then they heard another laugh. It was Agent G.B. "Welcome back!"

# Chapter 3
# LIVE

I'm sorry, Brody," Agent G.B. said with a chuckle. "The slide still needs some work."

Agent G.B. was on one of the screens. He was wearing a suit, tie, and really cool sunglasses too.

"Once you change back to your normal clothes, the oven mitt will come off," Agent G.B. said. "Well, I hope it will."

Brody crossed his arms. "Mm-hmm."

Jake was excited. They had finished two challenges already. They needed to complete one more to become Secret Slide Money Club agents.

"What is our next challenge?" he asked.

"Something strange is happening," Agent G.B. said. "Kids found stinky ads in their mailboxes this week. The ads are for Terry's Toy Store."

A picture of the ad went up on another screen.

"Marcus had one of those," Sophia said. She held her nose. "It smelled like dirty, wet socks."

"You are right," Agent G.B. said. "A lot of kids got one. Albatross is up to something."

"What?" Brody asked.

"I don't know," Agent G.B. said. "The kids are at the toy store right now."

Pictures of the kids at the toy store went up on the screen. Agent G.B. was right. There were a lot of kids.

"Look!" Sophia said. "There's Marcus!" She pointed at the screen. Marcus was holding his ad.

"Your third challenge will not be easy," Agent G.B. said. "Go to the toy store and stop Albatross's plan."

A Bible verse went up on one of the screens. "Remember this verse," Agent G.B. said.

*The wise have wealth and luxury, but fools spend whatever they get.*
*—Proverbs 21:20*

Sophia pulled out her notebook and wrote down the verse.

"Got it!" Sophia said.

Brody saw a backpack on the table. Next to it was a capsule. It said LIVE on the side.

"Is this for us?" Brody asked.

"Yes," Agent G.B. said. "That is the LIVE capsule."

Brody picked up the backpack and the LIVE capsule. He looked inside the capsule.

"The money in the LIVE capsule is all you can spend," Agent G.B. said. "When the money is gone, your spending stops. So you have to be smart about spending."

Sophia wrote in her notebook,

**When the money is gone, your spending stops.**
**Be smart about spending.**

"Make a spending plan and stick to it. Say no to impulse buying," Agent G.B. said.

"Did you say *pimples* buying?" Brody asked with a confused look.

"No, impulse buying. It sounds like this: *im-puls*," said Agent G.B.

"It means to buy something you did not plan on buying," Sophia said. She wrote,

**Make a spending plan.**
**Stick to it.**
**No impulse buying.**

Jake pointed at the screen. "Look! See the bracelet? An Albie!"

"I see him!" Brody said.

"You need to go," said Agent G.B. "The rocket car is ready for you."

"Yes!" Jake said. He turned to Brody. "High five . . . err . . . high mitt?"

"Not funny," Brody said.

Sophia jumped into the rocket car first. "It's my turn to drive."

"Aww! Come on!" said Jake and Brody.

"Get in and buckle up," Sophia said.

The boys jumped in the rocket car. Sophia pressed the start button.

*VROOOOOOM!*

Sophia softly pushed the gas pedal. But no flames came out this time. The rocket car moved slowly out of the headquarters.

"Really, Sophia?" Jake asked.

"It is smart to be safe," Sophia said with a smile.

# Chapter 4

# Buy More Toys

"Well, that was the slowest drive ever," Jake said.

"Don't get out until I turn the car off," Sophia said. They were at the toy store.

The three friends jumped out of the car. Brody was holding the backpack.

They could not believe their eyes. Kids were everywhere! And they were all holding stinky ads.

"Remember to keep your sunglasses on," Sophia said. "They cannot know who we really are."

"Glasses on," Jake said.

"EWWW!" Sophia said. "This place smells like dirty, wet socks. Look out for Albies."

"Look! There's Marcus!" Brody said. He pointed.

"Hey, Marcus!" yelled Jake.

Marcus came over. He was holding the envelope. The stinky ad was in it. "Do I know you?" he asked.

"I'm Agent Jake," Jake said. "This is Agent Sophia and Agent Brody."

"Well, we are not really agents yet," Brody said.

"What?" asked Marcus.

"Don't worry about it," Jake said. "We are with the Secret Slide Money Club."

"Hey, I have a Jake, Sophia, and Brody in my class," Marcus said.

"Umm . . . that's weird," Sophia said. "We are here to help you spend money the right way."

"Spend money the right way? What do you mean?" Marcus asked.

"We don't know yet," Sophia said. "But something will happen."

Brody pulled the LIVE capsule out of the backpack. He gave it to Marcus.

"This is for you. You can put your money in here," Brody said.

"I have forty dollars. I plan to buy *Super Dodgeball 3*. It costs thirty dollars," Marcus said.

Sophia pulled out her notebook. She wrote,

*Marcus has $40.*

*Super Dodgeball 3 costs $30.*

"Your plan is to buy only the game," Sophia said. "Don't spend the money on anything else. Or you won't have enough money for the game. Stick to the spending plan."

"Oh, I will," Marcus said.

Suddenly, there was a loud humming noise.

*HUMMMMMM!*

"What is that?" Jake asked.

The stinky ads started glowing red.

"Uh-oh," Sophia said. "They stink and they glow. That can't be good."

The kids holding the ads went into a daze. "Buy more toys," they all said.

The kids slowly walked into the store. They started picking up toys off the shelves.

"What is going on?" Brody asked.

"Marcus, you need to leave," Sophia said.

Marcus didn't say anything. He was in a daze too.

"Marcus?" Sophia said. "Marcus?"

"Buy more toys," Marcus said. He started walking toward the toy store.

"We have to stop this," Jake said. "The kids will spend all their money!"

Sophia nodded. "And Marcus won't have enough to buy his video game."

"Wait, Marcus!" Jake yelled.

Marcus did not turn around. He just walked into the store. "Buy more toys."

# Chapter 5
## Ad Airplanes!

Jake, Sophia, and Brody ran into the toy store. Kids were everywhere. They picked toys off the shelves, but they did not seem happy. They were dazed.

"Where did Marcus go?" Jake asked.

The three friends looked around the store. But they could not see Marcus. There were too many kids.

"Look at the cash register!" Sophia said.

There was a long line of kids buying toys.

"What is going on?" Jake asked.

Sophia began thinking. "Marcus's ad smelled like an Albie. Marcus went into a daze when his ad glowed red."

Sophia smiled. "I got it! Albatross did something to the ads. When you touch one, you go into a daze."

"And the kids now believe they must buy toys," Jake said.

"Impulse buying," Sophia said. "It hurts their spending plan."

Brody listened to the humming noise. *HUMMMMMM!*

He remembered something. "When the humming started, the ads glowed red," Brody said.

"We need to find where that humming is coming from," Jake said.

Sophia pointed. "Look! It's Marcus!" she yelled.

The three friends ran to Marcus. He had a football in his hand.

"Are you going to buy that?" Sophia asked.

Marcus nodded. "Buy more toys," he said.

"Cool football. I like it!" Jake said.

"No," Sophia said. "It's not cool. It's not part of the spending plan. It's an impulse buy."

Sophia took the football from Marcus. She looked at the price. It cost fifteen dollars. Sophia took out her notebook and wrote,

*Marcus has $40.*

*The football costs $15.*

*$40 – $15 = $25*

*Super Dodgeball 3 costs $30.*

Sophia showed Jake and Brody the notebook.

"If Marcus buys the football, he cannot buy *Super Dodgeball 3*!" Sophia said. "He will not have enough money."

"Yikes!" Brody said. "The football is an impulse buy. It messes up his spending plan."

Sophia gave Jake the football. "Get rid of this football," Sophia said.

Jake smiled. He threw the football over the shelves to the other side of the store.

"Wow. Nice throw," Brody said.

"Uh . . . you could have just put it back on the shelf," Sophia said.

Marcus ran off. "Must buy more toys!" he said.

"Ugh!" said Jake. "We need to stop him. He will run out of money."

The three friends started to chase Marcus, but then . . .

"LOOK OUT, JAKE!" Brody yelled.

Jake ducked. A red, glowing paper airplane just missed his head.

"What was that?" Jake asked.

The three friends turned around. There was an Albie. He had a bag full of red, glowing paper airplanes.

"Uh-oh," Sophia said. "I don't like this. He made airplanes out of the ads!"

"They are ad airplanes!" Brody said.

"This looks like trouble . . . with wings!" said Jake.

# Challenge Break!

Ad airplanes! Wow. I did not see that coming. Albies are sneaky.

Okay. Time for a break. And by break, I mean maze. Test your ad-airplane-dodging skills! If you run into an ad airplane, you have to start over. Good luck!

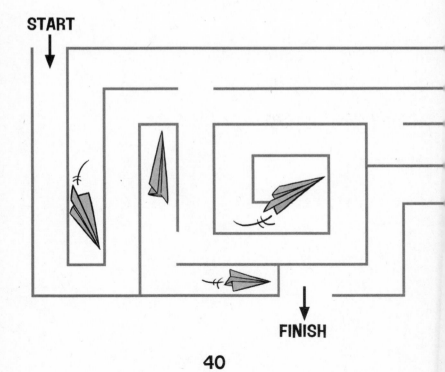

START

FINISH

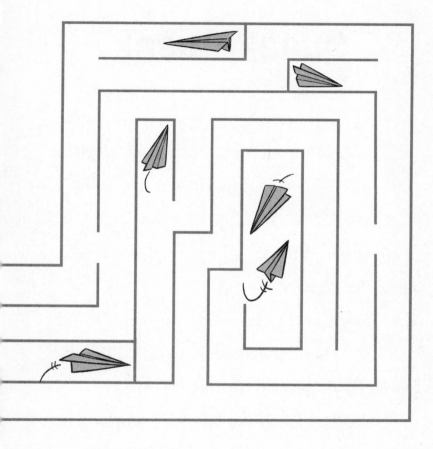

Did you make it? Awesome! Now let's see if Jake, Sophia, and Brody are as skilled as you!

# Chapter 6
# Quack Quack

The Albie grabbed another ad airplane out of his bag. He threw it at Sophia.

"AD AIRPLANE!" Jake yelled.

Sophia ducked. The ad airplane went over her head.

"What is the deal with throwing things today?" Sophia asked. "I did not like dodgeball, and I don't like this either!"

"Brody!" Jake yelled. "One is coming for you!"

An airplane almost hit Brody. The Albie was throwing a lot of airplanes now.

"Let's try to get away from him!" Brody said.

The three friends ran the other way. The Albie chased them. Jake saw a box full of toy cars.

"Let's see if he can get past this!" Jake said.

Jake pushed the box over. Toy cars went all over the floor. The Albie slipped on a car.

*WHOMP!!!* He fell down.

"Yes!" Brody said. They ran away from the Albie.

Then Sophia saw Marcus. "There's Marcus!" Sophia said.

The three friends stopped Marcus. He had a Sammy the Snuggly Snail in his hand.

"What are you doing with that?" Sophia asked.

"Buy more toys," Marcus said.

"Ugh. Can't you say something else?" Jake asked.

Brody looked at the toy.

"Hey, good pick!" Brody said. "Umm, not because I like Sammy the Snuggly Snail or anything."

"No! No!" Sophia said. "That is not a part of the spending plan. And we know you like Sammy the Snuggly Snail. Don't try to hide it."

Brody turned red.

Sophia looked at the price. The snail was twenty dollars. She wrote in her notebook,

*Marcus has $40.*

*Sammy the Snuggly Snail costs $20.*

*$40 – $20 = $20*

*Super Dodgeball 3 costs $30.*

Sophia showed Jake and Brody her notebook.

"Marcus won't have enough money if he buys the snail," Sophia said. "It's an impulse buy."

"Sophia is right," Jake said. "He needs to make a good money choice. That means not buying the snail."

Brody was bummed. "But look at it. Sammy the Snail is so snuggly."

Jake and Sophia shook their heads.

"The humming is really loud here," Jake said.

"You're right," said Sophia. She looked around. "I only see toys."

"Up there!" Jake said. He pointed to the top shelf.

There was a machine on the top shelf. It was making the humming noise.

"That is Albatross's machine!" Jake said. "We need to destroy it!"

Jake started climbing up the shelf.

"DUCK, JAKE!" Brody yelled.

Jake looked up. "I don't see a duck. Here, ducky ducky!"

An ad airplane hit Jake.

"Ugh," Brody said. "Not that kind of duck."

Jake climbed down the shelf.

"What are you doing, Jake?" Sophia asked.

Jake was in a daze. "Buy more toys," he said.

"Oh no," Sophia said.

# Chapter 7
# Game Over?

The Albie had caught up with the three friends.

"Ha! I'm back!" The Albie laughed.

"Oh, goody," Sophia said.

He threw some more ad airplanes. One went by Brody's head. It smelled really bad.

"ICK!!!" Brody said. "Those things really stink!"

Jake was still in a daze. He took a candy maker off the shelf. "Must buy more toys," he said.

"Hey, nice pick," said Brody.

"No! No! And no!" Sophia said. "Not a nice pick. He does not have any money."

Brody took the candy maker from Jake. "Sorry, Jake. You need your own LIVE capsule."

An ad airplane almost hit Sophia. "YIKES!" said Sophia "We must stop that machine."

"Right," Brody said.

Sophia and Brody started climbing up the shelves to the machine. The Albie kept throwing ad airplanes at them.

"This is really hard with an oven mitt," Brody said. "Hey, Sophia, look out!"

An ad airplane almost hit Sophia.

"Whew!" Sophia said. "That was close."

The Albie looked at Sophia. He was mad. "GRRRR! This one won't miss!"

The Albie threw an ad airplane really hard. It was too fast. Sophia could not get out of the way.

"HEY!" Sophia yelled as the ad airplane hit her hand.

Sophia fell off the shelves.

"Are you okay?" Brody asked.

Sophia did not look at Brody. She just looked at the toys on the shelves. "Buy more toys."

Brody sighed. "Oh no. You too?"

Brody was the only one left to stop the Albie and destroy the machine.

The Albie smiled. "Ha!" he said. "And this one is for you!"

The Albie pulled an ad airplane out of his bag. He threw it very hard. "GAME OVER!" he said.

The ad airplane flew right at Brody. "NOOOO!"

# Chapter 8
# Oven Mitts Are Awesome

"HI-YAHHHH!" Brody yelled.

He blocked the ad airplane with his oven mitt. The oven mitt was too thick for the ad airplane. It did not put Brody into a daze.

"Hey! Maybe this oven mitt is not so bad!" Brody said.

The Albie could not believe it. "GRRRR!" He began to throw more ad airplanes.

One by one, Brody blocked them all with his oven mitt. "This is a lot easier than dodging!"

Then Brody saw something on the shelf. It was a bunch of dodgeballs. He smiled.

"This time I will not lose dodgeball!" he said.

He grabbed some balls and jumped to the ground. He threw one at the Albie. The ball almost hit him.

"What?" said the Albie. He threw another ad airplane. Brody blocked it with his oven mitt.

"Not this time," Brody said. He threw another ball. The Albie ducked.

"Nice move," Brody said.

"Thank you," said the Albie.

Brody looked at the Albie's bag. It had one more ad airplane in it.

The Albie took the last ad airplane out of his bag. "GRRRR!"

Brody smiled. "It's time for this game to end," he said.

The Albie threw the ad airplane as hard as he could. Brody picked up a ball and threw it as hard as he could.

*BAMMM!!! CRUNCHHH!!!*

The ball hit the ad airplane. The ad airplane fell to the ground.

"ARGHHH!" the Albie yelled.

"Now it's GAME OVER," Brody said.

The Albie gave Brody an angry look.

"You don't have to do this. You can get free from Albatross," Brody said. "Let us help you follow the Master's Money Plan."

The Albie shook his head and ran away.

"Too bad," Brody said.

Just then, Brody saw Marcus. He was at the cash register with a lot of toys. He was going to buy them.

"Oh no!" Brody said. "Marcus won't have enough money to buy *Super Dodgeball 3*!"

# Chapter 9

# Marcus Gets His Game

Brody climbed up the shelves to the machine. He pushed it off.

*CRASHHHH!!!*

The machine hit the floor. It broke apart. The humming sound stopped. The ads stopped glowing red.

"It worked!" Brody said.

Jake and Sophia came out of the daze.

"Huh? What happened?" Jake asked.

"You two were hit by ad airplanes," Brody said.

Jake and Sophia saw the broken machine on the floor.

"How did you do that?" Sophia asked.

Brody grinned. "Let's just say I'm thankful for this oven mitt."

The kids in the store came out of the daze too. Brody looked at the counter. Marcus was still there.

"Come on. Marcus has a video game to buy!" Brody said.

The three friends picked out the game and went to Marcus.

"Here you go, Marcus!" Jake said. He handed him *Super Dodgeball 3*.

"Um, thanks. What happened?" Marcus asked.

"Albatross tried to get everyone to spend more than they should," Jake said. "He wanted us to make impulse buys."

"When you spend more than you should, you can't buy what you really want," Sophia said. "You have to be smart with spending. Make a spending plan, and stick to it."

Marcus took the money out of his LIVE capsule. He had forty dollars. He gave the game to the lady behind the counter.

"That will be thirty dollars," she said.

Marcus gave her his money.

"Here is your change," said the lady behind the counter. "You get ten dollars back."

"That's right," Sophia said. "You had forty dollars, but the game only cost thirty dollars. So you have ten dollars left."

"Cool!" Brody said. "What are you going to do with the ten dollars?"

Marcus smiled. He put the ten dollars in his LIVE capsule.

"I'm going to keep it in here," Marcus said, "so I have money when I want to buy another toy."

Brody smiled. "Like a Sammy the Snuggly Snail?"

"No," Marcus said. "Those are for little kids."

Brody turned red.

"Umm . . . yes . . . I know," Brody said. "I was just joking."

Jake and Sophia looked at Brody. They shook their heads.

The lady behind the counter gave Marcus his video game.

"Yes!" Marcus said. He was happy. "I have three friends coming over to my house tomorrow to play *Super Dodgeball 3*!"

Brody smiled. "I bet they are the coolest kids in the world."

Sophia ripped the Bible verse for the challenge out of her notebook.

***The wise have wealth and luxury, but fools spend whatever they get.***
***—Proverbs 21:20***

"Here you go, Marcus," Sophia said. She gave him the page from her notebook. "Be smart about spending. Make a spending plan, and stick to it."

Jake's eyes grew wide. "We just completed our third challenge!"

"Yes!" Brody said. He gave Jake a high five with his oven mitt. "High mitt!"

"Let's get back to headquarters," Sophia said. "And remember, I'm driving."

"Aww!" said Brody and Jake.

# Chapter 10

# Ice Cream Bars
# for Everyone!

Jake, Sophia, and Brody were back at the Secret Slide Money Club headquarters. Buttons were flashing and beeping. Agent G.B. was smiling on the screen.

"Great job!" he said.

"Albatross created a machine that made kids buy toys," Sophia said.

"Brody was able to destroy the machine and save Marcus and the kids at Terry's Toy Store," said Jake.

"Well, the slide helped by giving me an oven mitt," Brody said. He held up the oven mitt. "But I will be happy when it's off my hand."

"And it will be," Agent G.B. said. "Remember—money will run out. We must be smart with spending. The Albatross tempts kids to make impulse buys."

Now Agent G.B. had a big smile.

"Sophia, do you see that big green button in front of you?"

"Yes," Sophia said.

"Push it," Agent G.B. said.

"Umm . . . okay," Sophia said. She pushed the big green button.

Pictures of Jake, Sophia, and Brody came up on the screen. Next to Jake's picture, it said, "Agent Jake." Next to Sophia's picture, it said, "Agent Sophia." And next to Brody's picture, it said, "Agent Oven Mitt."

"Hey!" Brody said.

"Oh. Sorry," said Agent G.B. "Here you go."

The words changed. Now it said, "Agent Brody."

"That's better," Brody said.

"Congratulations, Jake, Sophia, and Brody!" Agent G.B. said. "You completed your third challenge. You are real Secret Slide Money Club agents!"

"YES!!!" the three agents yelled.

"You will rescue people from Albatross and help them follow the Master's Money Plan," said Agent G.B.

"Give—Save—Live," said Sophia.

"That's right," Agent G.B. said.

"You can count on us," said Jake.

"Brody, can you open that box?" Agent G.B. asked.

A box was sitting next to Brody. It was really cold.

"Wow," Brody said. "This box is freezing. Good thing I have my oven mitt."

He opened the box.

"YESSSS!" Brody yelled.

He reached in with his oven mitt and pulled out three chocolate-dipped ice cream bars.

"Ice cream party!" Brody said.

Everyone laughed.

"Welcome to the Secret Slide Money Club," Agent G.B. said. "And get ready. The challenges have only begun."

# Your Money Challenge

High five! Or if you have an oven mitt on, high mitt! You finished the third book.

Can you believe it? Jake, Sophia, and Brody are real Secret Slide Money Club agents. That's pretty cool.

But wait. It is not over. You need to complete your own Money Challenge.

Secret Slide Money Club agents have a spending plan. And they stick to it. So here is your Money Challenge. . . .

First, make sure you have three capsules—GIVE, SAVE, and LIVE. You can make these on your own. Put money in each one in the right order (PSSSST!!! It's GIVE—SAVE—LIVE).

Then make a spending plan for the money in your LIVE capsule. Plan how you will spend the money. You can put the plan on a sheet of paper.

Show your parents. They will think it's SOOOO cool. Because it is.

Keep following the Master's Money Plan!

Okay. The book is over. You can close it now.

Wait! Not yet.

Just kidding. The book is done.

GAME OVER!

# About the Author

Art Rainer is an Albatross fighter. He helps people make good money choices (Give—Save—Live) so they will not become smelly, mean Albies. Art is the author of *The Money Challenge: 30 Days of Discovering God's Design for You and Your Money*. He is married to Sarah and has three sons—Nathaniel, Joshua, and James.